# FOOL'S DEMISE

## *A Western Adventure*

## A.T. BUTLER

# CHAPTER ONE

Jacob Payne, the most legendary bounty hunter in the Arizona Territory, was up to his elbows in hot water and suds. He had noticed one of the other women in Bonnie Loft's boarding house smirk at him when she walked by a few minutes earlier, but he wasn't at all ashamed to be working in the kitchen. He had been invited to dinner by his sweetheart, and was eager to use the opportunity to both show her how much he appreciated her and show her landlady that he wasn't as worthless as she thought he was.

If that meant washing the dishes after a meal for six people, he was happy to do that.

Jacob used a sponge to scrub at the caked-on crust of bread from the heavy pan. Unused to holding such slippery things, he lost his grip and dropped the dish into the water. He hopped back awkwardly, as he accidentally splashed greasy, soapy water onto his shirt.

"Blast," he said under his breath as he looked down to see the damage. Oh well. He shrugged. It would dry.

"You're sure you don't want an apron?" a kind voice said from behind him.

Jacob glanced over his shoulder to see Bonnie, leaning with one shoulder against the doorframe and watching him amusedly.

"Naw. A little water and soap never hurt me."

"That grease might set, though."

"Oh." Jacob looked down at his shirt again. "Well ... It was probably time to get a new one anyway."

Bonnie laughed. "What a simple solution."

Jacob caught up the last of the dirty silverware and began to scrub. "You'll have to come with me when I go shopping. A lady of taste like yourself can help make sure I only get the best."

"I'm sure I can find the time to do that."

The two gazed warmly at each other from across the room. Jacob had been courting Bonnie for a couple months now. He had worried that maybe he was going to slow for her, but with the pain and memory of his first wife's death still lingering, he didn't want to rush into any hasty decision.

But now, with the weather in Tucson finally cooling and feeling something like what Jacob remembered to be autumn, the season was nearing its end and so was that chapter in his life. Though he didn't know yet when or where it would happen, Jacob was slowly forming the plan in his mind to propose to this beautiful, kind woman.

Bonnie Loft was a better person that Jacob could have ever hoped for. She was generous with others; she was patient with him. And above all, she was understanding. It must not be easy for her to be courted by a man who left town constantly, a man she never knew if or when he would be around. A man she couldn't always count on to be there. But she understood that he was doing his job, and she unwaveringly supported his need to do so.

He needed a woman who was even-keeled and compassionate. One who accepted that he would just buy a new shirt, rather than fret about ruining his other one.

Jacob thanked God every day that he had found his way to Tucson and that he had met Bonnie Loft. And that some other man hadn't already snatched her up. He couldn't quite believe his luck. The bounty hunter didn't quite know what she saw in him, but he was determined to be better for her every day if he could. She was more than worth it.

And doing a tub full of dishes was a simple way to show his thanks.

He just wished his hands weren't all wet so he could take her in his arms.

"You're not done yet?" Mrs. Withers demanded as she walked in to the kitchen. She shook her head, disappointed. "I knew should have done this myself. You'll be here all night struggling to do this simple chore, and I won't get a wink of sleep until you're gone."

"I'm just about done, ma'am," he said, rinsing the last of the forks. "I've just got to dry these and put them away and then I'll be out of your hair."

She huffed, frustrated. "I don't know that I want you poking around my kitchen, Mr. Payne. Seems not right to allow a stranger that much access into my private domain."

"I'll help him," Bonnie volunteered, stepping forward. "He can dry. I'll put them all away. Then we'll be done even sooner and Jacob doesn't have to go looking for anything you don't want him to see."

Jacob wisely kept his mouth shut. Mrs.

Withers had never liked him, but she put up with him for Bonnie's sake. He needed to let her handle the landlady; he would follow whatever plan the two women came up with.

Mrs. Withers pursed her lips, looked Jacob up and down, and then around at the kitchen. "Very well, Bonnie," she said finally with a sigh. "If you see that this man doesn't get into anything he's not meant to, I suppose I don't mind if he does a little more work around here. No lollygagging, though. It's past nine o'clock, and he needs to be gone as soon as you all are done. Mind you two don't even think about any shenanigans. I'll be right over there in the sitting room, chaperoning."

"Never," Jacob said solemnly.

Bonnie grinned at him behind Mrs. Withers's back.

The older woman tutted and left them alone.

Bonnie pulled a fresh towel from the drawer under the window and handed it to Jacob. "Remember. No lollygagging, sir," she said with a wink.

Jacob laughed and picked up the first of the clean plates to dry off.

"I appreciate you helping me."

She laughed. "Oh, goodness. It's nothing.

Not only did I get to spend the evening with you, and make sure you get a good home-cooked meal, but I also got out of doing the dishes myself. Honestly, Jacob, there really isn't any other way I'd want to spend tonight."

He handed her the first plate and reached for the second one. "I didn't want to say anything in front of your friends," he said, "but I wonder if you have any plans on Sunday after church."

Bonnie smiled. "None at all. You'll be in Tucson this Sunday, Jacob?"

He nodded. "I will, and I was hoping I could escort you to church, and then to the Santos home after."

"Santos?" She looked taken aback. "Marshal Santos?"

"He and his wife would like us to come over for Sunday dinner, if you don't have any other engagements."

"Well ... I ..." She trailed off.

Jacob hid his smile. It wasn't often that he was able to so surprise Bonnie that she was at a loss for words, but he was pleased that such an invite had that effect.

"If it's too much, we don't have to go."

"No, it's not that. It's just ... I just never thought in all my days I would warrant an invite from a U.S. Marshal. It's ... It's a lot to get used to."

"Well, you deserve it. You're a favorite around this town, and not just with me. It's only right that the Santoses notice too."

"I'm sure you're overstating it, but thank you. I'd be happy to go. But ... I do have one question."

"What's that?" He handed her another dry plate.

"Have you ever actually had a meal with the marshal when he didn't start talking about some outlaw you needed to track down?"

Jacob paused, giving the question good thought. "You know ... I'm not sure I have."

Bonnie nodded. "All right. Then ..." She smiled brightly. "Then I guess I'll just expect a lot of business talk over dinner. And maybe we'll be surprised otherwise."

She turned away to put the stack of dinner plates back on the shelf where she had collected them earlier that night.

"That's a good thought," Jacob said, gently. "And even if he does have a job for me, at least we'll have gotten to attend church together and have dinner."

"That's true." Bonnie crossed the room to him, put a hand on his arm and leaned close.

"And when you go out again, to hunt down another dangerous man, I'll be so proud of you. Like I always am."

Jacob's heart thumped. He smiled down at her. "Come on. Let's finish up these dishes, so you can walk me to the door and we can do some lollygagging on the front porch."

# CHAPTER TWO

Sunday afternoon, after a moving sermon from Pastor Ambrose about loving your neighbor, Jacob escorted Bonnie to the home of the U.S. Marshal, Owen Santos, and his wife, Marguerite.

The Santoses had lived in Tucson for more than ten years already, building their adobe home little by little over time, until the finished structure stood before them. It was not over-large but spread out luxuriously in a single story, with a wing of rooms on either side and a small courtyard guiding guests to the front door. It was the kind of home they could be proud of to live in for many years to come.

The couple walked up the front path, past several cacti that had been allowed to flourish, to where Jacob knocked on the wide wooden door.

The marshal himself answered the door, throwing it wide for his guests. "Payne, Bonnie. Good to see you both. Mrs. Santos and I are glad you could make it."

Jacob had only met Mrs. Santos once before, when the woman had brought a batch of freshly baked cookies to the Tucson jail to treat the deputies. Though not a deputy himself, Jacob happened to be there at the time and was much impressed with her. Marguerite Santos seemed to be slightly older than her husband, though gladly and easily falling into the supportive background behind him. From everything Jacob had heard, Mrs. Santos seemed to make it her life's work to make her husband's life as easy as possible.

She came forward to meet her guests, drawing Bonnie in for a hug and letting Jacob take her hand.

"Thank you for coming," she said warmly. "I've been pestering Owen to invite you for weeks."

"It's just us," the marshal said, directing his guests into the sitting room. "I believe my deputies have had quite enough of me on a daily basis, and Mrs. Santos wanted a chance to get to know you."

"Me?" Jacob said, as he took his seat next to Bonnie.

"Of course you. She's heard so much about you but has barely spoken to you. I did, of course, point out to her that you're often not even in Tucson. She made me promise that I wouldn't let you out of the city until after Sunday dinner."

Jacob laughed. "A reasonable request."

"Is there anything I can help with?" Bonnie asked hopefully.

"No, ma'am. Thank you, but I know that you're waiting on people hand and foot the rest of the week. Today let us take care of you for a bit."

Santos smiled at her from his seat across the room. Jacob could smell whatever was cooking for supper waft in from the kitchen. Though he couldn't be rightly sure from this distance, he caught the scent of onions, butter, rosemary and a few other things. Not for the first time did Jacob think it might be nice to have his own kitchen, his own little wife preparing a roast for him when he came home, or when he invited his friends over for Sunday dinner at his own house. The boarding house he was currently staying in left much to be desired.

Soon, he reminded himself.

"I'm so sorry," Mrs. Santos said, standing in the doorway and wiping her hands in her apron. "I need another set of hands. Owen, do you think you could—"

"I'll go," said Bonnie, standing and already walking across the room before anyone could object. "Please. I love to cook. Let me."

Both Jacob and the marshal had stood when she did. They glanced at each other; Jacob shrugged lightly as though to withdraw any objection, and the marshal responded.

"If you're sure, I won't stop you." He held his hands up as though surrendering.

"You men enjoy your time," she said before following Mrs. Santos into the kitchen.

Both men sat again watching her leave, and the marshal immediately changed the subject of conversation.

"What's the hold up, Payne?"

Jacob blinked at him and frowned. "Sir? I'm sorry— I thought ... Were you waiting on something from me?"

"I'm not. But Miss Loft might be."

"Oh, yes." Jacob looked down and picked at

the seam of his trousers before looking up again. "Soon. I was just thinking about it."

"So, what's the hold up?" the marshal asked, more gently this time.

"I'm not sure. I ... You know I was married before?"

Santos nodded.

"Louisa and our son both died after taking ill and maybe ... Maybe I'm afraid of that happening again. I don't know."

"You know that was entirely different circumstances. That was just after the war, after all."

"Yes, but I was still away from home a lot. Like I am now. I know I need to get over these fears, Marshal. I will. I am."

"You take too long, Payne, and someone else will see what a treasure she is."

"I know."

The men sat thoughtfully for another moment before Mrs. Santos called them in for dinner. Jacob was grateful for the marshal's interest in his happiness, but also grateful to be interrupted so he didn't need to try to defend himself any further.

The four adults sat down around the dinner table, the marshal said grace, and then they proceeded to enjoy one of the best roasts Jacob had had the pleasure of being served since he got to the territory.

In between bites, Jacob entertained the table with stories from his time in Valencia and Olmos. As a bounty hunter, sometimes Jacob got to see even more of the underbelly of a town than the marshal might.

"While we're on the subject," the marshal said, "I wonder if I can interest you in a small job this week?"

Bonnie and Jacob exchanged a meaningful look. She winked at him, and Jacob felt all his apprehension at leaving her dissipate. She understood. She always understood.

"Come on, Marshal. You know that the size of the job won't deter me. If a man needs to be caught, I'll catch him. What kind of job is it?"

"There's a man—a kid really. Not sure he even has to shave, come to think of it. This kid seems to have it in his head he's a great gambler, but every time he loses, which is often, he ends up losing his temper and stealing back his cash at gunpoint."

"Well, that's a shame," Jacob said. "I hate seeing someone that young turn to crime."

"He hasn't hurt anyone yet, but from the stories I'm hearing it's just a matter of time. I need you to go find him and stop him. And if you can recover any of the winnings, I'd appreciate it."

"Seems strange that anyone would offer a reward for this."

The marshal nodded. "I know, but it seems this kid has wrangled with wrong man at last. I don't know how many times he has pulled this stunt, but this last week he stole five hundred dollars off Joseph Meyer."

"Meyer? As in the owner of the largest gold mine in the White Mountains? That Joseph Meyer?"

"That's the one. Not only does Meyer have the money to put up for an award, he's also the kind of man that leans heavily on principle. Even if this ends up costing him money and time and energy, he still wants the kid to be punished. Both for the kid's own sake but also as a lesson to anyone else paying attention."

"Well..." Jacob took a deep breath, thinking about everything he had been told about Meyer. He was the kind of rich man from New York that could have easily paid someone to manage his interests in the Arizona Territory, but had come himself. "The world needs men of principle, there's no doubt about that."

"Glad you agree. It's not going to be exciting

or all that difficult to capture this kid, but it needs to be done."

"Do you have a name?"

"Billy Watts. I've got a description here somewhere..." The marshal patted his pockets looking for the folded piece of paper that he pulled out to read from. "About five-foot-six. Thin, light brown hair. Blue eyes and freckles."

"Any idea where I should start once I get up there?"

"The last I heard Watts was in Blackville, but I think he moves around a lot. Probably start there, though. Maybe they'll have heard more about him."

Jacob nodded and started thinking about how soon he could leave and what he needed to do before he was gone. The White Mountains weren't close, and if he was going to be away from Tucson for weeks, he had a lot to think about.

# CHAPTER THREE

The next day, Bonnie was as good as her word. Though she was needed at the San Xavier Cafe for her job as a waitress by the dinner hour, in the morning beforehand she accompanied Jacob to the general store to choose a new shirt. He found a soft fabric in dark colors, and purchased enough for two new shirts.

While the pair walked farther down the street to the seamstress, Bonnie tried to talk Jacob into letting her sew it for him.

"Are you worried I won't do a good job?" she teased.

"No, I'm worried you won't get any sleep. I appreciate the offer. I really do, and your help today has been exactly what I needed. But if you're going to be at the cafe the rest of the day, when will you have time to sew a shirt?"

"All right," she relented easily. "But this is something I'd like to be able to do for you in the future. If you'll allow me."

"I'm sure that day will come eventually," he said.

After placing his rush order with Miss Holliday—she'd have both shirts ready for him to collect in the morning—Jacob walked Bonnie to the cafe and then ran the rest of his errands before leaving town.

Later that night he found himself in the Golden Saddle Saloon. Jacob was never much of a gambler, but the friends and company he enjoyed at that watering hole brought him back again and again.

Lucky and Abe were holding court at their usual table in the corner. Professional gamblers, they were just good enough to win regularly and avoid having to find any other work, but just smart enough to let the other Tucson residents and visitors win occasionally too. Abe had confided to Jacob that they had been getting tired of having to move to new towns whenever they won all the money from everyone else who lived there. They seemed to be content to lose often enough here in Tucson to be able to stay put longer.

"Should I deal you in, Payne?" Abe asked as he saw the bounty hunter approaching.

"Nope. Not me." Jacob had grabbed a beer from Pete the bartender, made his way across the full room and leaned against the wall by where the men were sitting. "I'm heading out tomorrow and just want to relax a bit tonight. You know I'm never quite good enough to beat you."

Mondays tended to be busy nights for the Golden Saddle Saloon. After behaving themselves at home all day on Sundays, many men wanted to reward themselves as soon as possible the next day. With as many people as were in the saloon that night, laughing, chatting and having a good time, Jacob knew he would have a hard time being part of the conversation if he didn't sit down at the table. Nevertheless, he still preferred to stay out of the game and just enjoy the time as it was with these men.

"Suit yourself." Abe shrugged. "Where you off to?"

"You leaving Bonnie again?" Jacob's one other good friend in town, Edwin Hogg, never missed an opportunity to tease him about that.

"Think I could take her to supper one of these nights?"

Jacob refused to rise to the bait. "Miss Bonnie Loft is her own person and can spend her evenings with whoever she chooses ... But I would probably drop dead with shock if she chose you."

The other men, including Edwin, all laughed. They were happy he had met such a fine woman, and he suspected when he wasn't around they all wondered the same thing the marshal had brought up the previous day.

"I'm heading east," Jacob said, picking up the thread of Abe's question. "East and north to the White Mountains. I don't have much of a lead just yet, so I may be awhile if I have to spend some time sniffing out the fella."

"White Mountains?" The younger man across the table from Abe spoke up. Jacob thought his name might be Matt or Martin, but he hadn't ever officially met him. "You know it's cold up there this time of year, don't ya? Someone told me this was your first winter in Tucson. Is that right?"

"Sure is. It's about time I have use for the heavy coat I brought out from Virginia. I was despairing of it ever getting below fifty degrees here."

"Oh, it'll get even colder in a month or so," the young man said. "I've lived around this territory most of my life. It may only last a few weeks, but especially if you're going to mountains, you'll be glad you have that coat."

"Speaking of the mountains," Edwin said, nodding toward the door. "Didn't Pierce just come back from there?"

Jacob looked up to where he indicated and saw the bounty hunter Clifford Pierce entering the saloon. The man was a few inches shorter than Jacob, with ashy brown hair and a face in need of a shave. Otherwise, he was unremarkable and, Jacob had to admit, probably did an excellent job blending into the crowd when hunting for outlaws.

The other man caught Jacob's eye and saw him watching. Without acknowledging, Pierce made his way to the bar and leaned over to speak to the bartender.

"You've met Pierce, right?" Edwin asked.

Jacob glanced down at his friend still seated at the table and couldn't help but grin at his teasing smile. Yes, Jacob had met Pierce. Jacob had even saved the man's life, but that wasn't the sort of thing he wanted to hold over the other bounty hunter. Nonetheless, he thought if Pierce had been up in the White Mountains he might just have the kind of information Jacob was looking for.

He should at least ask.

"Think I'll go say hi," Jacob said, making his excuses and leaving the poker table.

He wove through the crowd of drinking and riotous men back to where Pete, the bartender, was bringing Pierce a whiskey. As he set it down on the wood surface, Jacob called out.

"Good to see you, Pierce."

Clifford turned around, drink in hand and without taking his eyes off Jacob, downed the whole glass like a shot.

"Can I get you another?" Jacob asked, eyeing the empty glass.

"Nah, I'll get it." Clifford turned back around to the bar, spoke to Pete and then gave Jacob his attention. "Something you need, Payne?"

Jacob felt a flash of temper at the other man's rudeness, but reminded himself to be the bigger man. If Pierce wanted to be sullen and resentful over what Jacob had done for him, that was his own soul he was poisoning and didn't really hurt Jacob any.

He cleared his throat. "Heard you recently came back from the White Mountains."

"Yep." Clifford leaned back against the bar,

with both elbows up and behind him, taking up as much space as possible.

"I'm heading off there myself tomorrow. I wonder if you heard anything about a Billy Watts. Gambler. Kid, most likely."

Clifford laughed; it seemed almost torn out of him, as though he couldn't help himself in spite of his efforts. "Billy?" He grinned and raised his eyebrows. "Billy Watts is wanted now, is he?"

"He is. Marshal Santos asked me to go take a look, but I suppose if you want to join—"

"No, no." Clifford waved his hands off, denying any offer Jacob was about to make him. Pete returned at that moment with a beer for the bounty hunter, and he took a long draught before he said anything else. "I'll tell you what I know, but I'm not even going to bother. That boy is a fool and a fool with a gun is more dangerous than the most blood-thirsty murderer."

"Yeah, Santos didn't know much but I didn't think I was looking for a professional at all."

Pierce just continued to laugh. "I'm sorry." He started to cough, choking on his beer. "No, not a professional. Gimme a second and I'll tell you what I know. Have a seat."

He gestured to the stool next to him, only

recently vacated, and Jacob sat. Truth be told, Pierce's reaction worried him a bit, but he still determined to bring the kid in. If the marshal had asked it of him, it must be important.

Clifford took another long draw on his beer, cleared his throat, and sat up straight, placing both palms on the bar.

"So, this kid—Billy Watts. I was in ..." Clifford looked up at the ceiling as though the answer was written there. "Lawrence it was."

"Lawrence, Arizona," Jacob repeated.

"Right. But he won't be there anymore. Anyway, I was in Lawrence following the trail of a horse thief and thought I'd spend the night playing some cards. You understand. Relax a bit."

"Sure."

"Now, mind you, I wasn't in the same game as this Watts fellow, so I didn't hear the whole conversation, but after a bit there was some yelling and shoving started, Watts waving his gun around and threatening until he had the attention of everyone in the place."

"Did he shoot anyone?"

Clifford shook his head. "Not that night. But, it's only a matter of time, if he hasn't since I seen him. You know the type."

Jacob nodded.

"Right. Man feels so victimized and out of control he thinks his only option is a show of force."

"Boy that age hasn't had a chance to learn better."

"You got that right. But, luckily, that night the man he was yelling at did know better. Or at least knew to value his life more than his wallet. He gave the kid what he was demanding and got him to leave without bothering anyone else. Soon as he got out of the door we heard gunshots and a couple thuds, like the kid fired at the ground in his temper tantrum." He shook his head.

"That makes at least the second time he's done that, far as I know."

"Oh, I've heard more like five or six," Clifford said. "Course most of that is just rumor, but I wouldn't be surprised. I didn't hear where he went off to, but he left Lawrence that night or the next morning. Someone there might be able to point you in the right direction. Is there really a bounty on the kid?"

Jacob nodded. "One of his victims is a rich man of principle."

"Well," Clifford said after draining his beer

glass. "If the world had more of those you and I would be out of a job."

Jacob couldn't agree more.

# CHAPTER FOUR

It took Jacob and his horse Blaze a full week to make their way east and north into the White Mountains. Another month or so and he'd be dealing with snow, and it would be even slower going. Jacob made a promise to himself to be back in Tucson before Christmas.

The last time he had been on this side of the territory, Jacob had been gifted Blaze from a grateful farmer whose daughter Jacob had helped rescue. He almost wished he had time to visit that family again, but the town of Elk Springs wasn't anywhere near Lawrence and where he was going.

As he rode through the foothills and the forests that climbed the slope of the White Mountains, Jacob had plenty of time to consider his first task on the job. If there had ever been an outlaw that he wanted to be sure to bring in alive, it was Billy Watts. From everything Jacob had learned, he seemed to be just a naive kid who needed some guidance.

Jacob spent a week in and out of small Arizona towns, occasionally staying overnight in a real hotel, or getting a real bath. But most of his week of travel was on the road, catching quick meals as he could and alone with his thoughts.

The last night before Jacob got to Lawrence, he rode as far as he could before it got dark and made camp. With so long on the road, he was feeling a little impatient, and wished he could go to sleep that night without having to build a fire. The cold mountain night forced his hand, and Jacob finally was able to fall asleep with his heavy wool coat wrapped around him.

After a quick bite at his camp, Jacob was up and on the road again early in the morning the next day. Though he had been able to find some towns along the way that would offer him a bed, a bath, and a hot meal, traveling that distance from Tucson, a couple hundred miles to the mountains, was a big investment for him. Jacob began to wonder if he should maybe not settle in Tucson, being so far south in the territory.

Maybe moving a bit north would be better for his work.

He wondered what Bonnie would feel about that.

The bounty hunter pushed the concern from his mind as he approached the edge of Lawrence. It was mid-morning, with citizens, wagons and horses filling the streets.

Jacob had had plenty of time to think about where the first place he should start his investigation. If Billy Watts had been in Lawrence but left it, it was unlikely he had left on foot. Which means one of the last places he must have gone was the livery.

Jacob and Blaze rode down the main street of Lawrence, straight toward the livery stationed near the end of the street. It seemed all but empty. Even after dismounting, no waiting assistance came to meet him.

"Hello?" he called.

"Coming!"

Jacob peered into the dark recesses of the stable toward where he heard the voice. He thought, he suspected, that the voice was—

A small, wiry woman in trousers and tall boots came striding out to meet him. She wiped her hands on the front of her dark, loose-fitting shirt, and tucked a loose curl behind one ear with one hand, while reaching to shake Jacob's hands with the other.

"Sorry about that," she said. "You're the first person to come by all morning and I was getting some long-neglected chores done. Name's Rebecca Jones. Call me Beck. And who's this?"

She gestured to Blaze, with an admiring look in her eye, but knew better than to approach such a strong creature without letting him at least get a whiff of her.

"Blaze. And I'm Jacob Payne. Wanted to ask you some questions actually, if you've got a minute, Mrs. Jones."

He watched Beck carefully as she interacted with Blaze. She seemed to be about Jacob's own age, and in no way self-conscious about the fact that she was a woman in a primarily man's world. In fact, if Jacob had to put a point on it, he might even guess she was proud of her role. Of course, maybe that kind of pride was what it took to get through some men's thick skulls who might not think her up to it. But, despite the fact that Beck was barely over five-feet, maybe a full twelve inches shorter than Jacob, she appeared more than up to the task of wrangling a two-thousand-pound animal.

"Not missus. Miss Jones. But, really, call me Beck. Please." She stroked Blaze's neck softly. "Everyone else around here does. I know your momma probably raised you different, but I reckon if you're careful to say it respectfully, there's no harm in it. Now, what questions did you have for me. Do we need to get this handsome fella out of his saddle?"

"We should. Yes."

"I'll do that. It's my job, after all. You talk. Follow me."

Jacob grinned to himself as Beck led the horse away, into the stable to take care of everything he needed. With the animal taken care of, Jacob could turn his attention to finding the trail of Billy Watts.

"I'm looking for a boy, a young man, that was here recently. Maybe a couple weeks ago now. Billy Watts."

"Billy Watts?" she murmured to herself as she went about her tasks.

"My understanding is he left here in a huff or temper after stealing some cash at the poker table."

She laughed, a deep throaty rumble from deep in her belly. "Oh yes. I remember. Billy. He threatened me with that little pistol of his, too. Seemed to think frightening me out of my wits in the middle of the night was the best way to get a horse saddled and ready more quickly. Foolish child. I heard all about him."

"Did he happen to say where he was going from here?"

She peered at him over her shoulder, finally giving Jacob as close of a look as she had given his horse.

"He did. Wouldn't shut up about it as a matter of fact. Seems like any person you asked in this town would know the answer to that."

"Really?" Jacob frowned. How could everyone else in Lawrence know the one detail that Clifford Pierce managed to miss?

"Absolutely. I don't know if the kid thought he was ... I dunno. Somehow provoking someone into challenging him, or hoping someone would come after him or just trying to look like a bigger deal than he actually is. But he said over and over that he'd be going down to Raton and that nobody better follow him."

Jacob couldn't help but let out a groan. Raton was one of the towns he had stopped in for a mid-day meal on his way to Lawrence. It hadn't even occurred to him to ask about Billy Watts since he was still several days away. And now he had gone almost a week out of his way.

"Not what you were hoping to hear, is it?" Beck asked kindly.

Jacob shook his head. They stood silently together for another moment while Jacob thought about what to do next.

"Did you want me to saddle this boy up again for you?"

"No." Jacob sighed. "He deserves a good rest, don't you think?"

"I do." She patted Blaze's flank. "He's a gorgeous creature and deserves the best."

"Well, too bad for him he's stuck with me."

Beck laughed, continuing to brush down the horse. "Anything else I can do for you right now?"

"Well ... any suggestion for how to spend the rest of my day? I figure I'll give Blaze a good rest and get started back on down the hill in the morning."

"It's really too bad you came all the way up here. But, since you're here I might suggest you head over to the diner. They got their annual apple pie these last few weeks, and I don't think I'm overstating it to say that it will change your life."

Jacob had a flash of memory, of Bonnie bringing him a slice of apple pie at the San Xavier Cafe in Tucson. "I'll look into it. But, while I'm here I should also probably get as much information about Billy Watts as there is to be had. Do you happen to know where he was staying, or even who he was playing cards with that night?"

"I couldn't say for sure, but there's only one hotel here in Lawrence so far. The Larkspur Hotel off on Larkspur Street. Just head back that way—" she pointed along the main street "—and take a left up there a bit. You'll see it. Two stories with a deep porch on the right side. The Schmidts run it and they're pretty friendly with the law. If that Billy character stayed with them they're as like as not to tell you what they know."

Jacob thanked the woman and made his way back through Lawrence to the Larkspur Hotel. If he was going to give Blaze the rest he deserved, the bounty hunter would need to find a place to sleep for the night anyway.

Beck's directions had been spot-on; the Larkspur Hotel loomed over the narrow street close to the road and demanding the attention of passersby. A young woman, maybe mid-twenties, swept the porch as he approached.

"Good morning," she said cheerily once she realized he was coming to her establishment. "You looking for a room?"

Jacob climbed the steps to the hotel. "I am. And I'd like to talk to the owner if he's around."

"You're talking to her," she replied with a mischievous grin. "Or one of them. Come in. I'll call my husband and we'll get you settled, answer your questions. Whatever you need."

Carrying her broom inside, and leaving the porch clean and welcoming for their next guest, the woman led the way into the hotel.

"I'm Mrs. Schmidt," she said over her shoulder to him. "What brings you to Lawrence?" As she made her way behind the front desk of her hotel, she rang the call bell announcing their presence.

"I came looking for someone—I'm a bounty hunter and the marshal asked me special. But it seems I'm too late to catch the man. It's actually why I was hoping to speak to you and your husband. I'm told the man I was looking for likely stayed here."

The door to the back office opened at that moment, and a man at least two decades his wife's senior entered. Mr. Schmidt's face lit up when he saw a potential customer and immediately set to work welcoming Jacob.

"Welcome, welcome. You'd like a room? How long will you be staying with us?" His pen was poised above the ledger, waiting to record whatever Jacob said.

"Jacob Payne. Just tonight, thanks. I was just

asking your wife about a previous guest you might have had. I wonder if either of you remember a Billy Watts, from probably a couple weeks ago now."

Mrs. Schmidt rolled her eyes. "Billy? Skinny little thing? Yes, I remember him."

"He do it again?" Mr. Schmidt asked.

"Well, let's just say there's a reason I'm looking for him. I'm a bounty hunter, sir."

"I heard he got more than fifty dollars off that gentleman at the saloon that night," Mr. Schmidt said. "And then left us here with an unpaid bill."

Jacob shook his head. "Yeah, that about squares with what I've been hearing as well."

"Well," Mrs. Schmidt said with a sigh, "let's get you settled in your room for the night, and then you can ask us all the questions you want. We don't want to leave you standing around the lobby forever."

## CHAPTER FIVE

Though Jacob planned to leave Lawrence, Arizona Territory, early the next morning, he still had almost a full day to spend in town. Mr. Schmidt showed him to his room in the Larkspur Hotel just before suppertime. It was small, but private and cozy. Jacob gave himself a few minutes to wash up and relax before he did anything else, even to taking off his boots.

He didn't quite feel right lying in the bed in the middle of the day, but he had to admit that even having a bed was a nice change. As he went about getting settled in his hotel room, Jacob went over what he knew about his quarry.

Clifford Pierce had directed him here to the White Mountains, but now Jacob had learned that Billy Watts wasn't here at all, and hadn't been for quite some time. Jacob couldn't help but wonder if Pierce had known that. Would that man have lied to Jacob's face? He was used to outlaws and criminals—men afraid of justice—lying and misleading, but would another bounty hunter? Was there a reason Pierce would have let Jacob think something that wasn't true, and let the outlaw elude his grasp?

Jacob didn't want to jump to any conclusions about the lawman, but he certainly would feel better once he was on the road again. He even thought for a split second about renting a fresh horse from Beck and leaving right away, but he didn't want to do that to Blaze.

So instead, Jacob changed into his only clean shirt, smoothed down his cowlick on the back of his head, and headed back downstairs to talk to the Schmidts. Both stood behind the front desk talking quietly and looked up when he came down the steps.

"You getting hungry there, Mr. Payne?" Mr. Schmidt asked. "The price of your room includes breakfast, but we're happy to include you in our supper plans now if you've a mind."

"I don't want to put you out. Beck— Miss Jones over at the livery suggested I try the diner—"

"Oh, no! Stay here. Do, please," Mrs.

Schmidt said eagerly. "I made more than enough and we'd like to be able to help you with your search if we can."

"All right," Jacob agreed easily. "I'm mighty grateful to you, ma'am."

"Come this way."

Mrs. Schmidt led them to a small dining room just off the entry of the hotel. Like his bedroom upstairs, Jacob found the dining hall small but cozy, and wished he could take the time for a leisurely cup of coffee and maybe a newspaper in the morning. But, of course, he couldn't let Watts get any farther ahead.

"You two just sit," she said, indicating the table nearest the window, "and I'll get everything taken care of."

Following his host, Jacob took a grateful seat. "This is quite an improvement from a cold biscuit over coals that I had for breakfast this morning."

"Have you been on the road long?"

"About a week. I came all the way from Tucson, and I'll have to go all the way back."

"Really?" Mr. Schmidt frowned. "Seems to me most bounty hunters I've heard of don't stay put in one place."

"I've, uh ... I've found a beautiful reason to stick close to the town."

"Ah, yes." He grinned. "I'm familiar with reasons like that. I have a similar reason to be here. I would have been perfectly happy staying in Maryland, but when Mrs. Schmidt and I married a few years ago it was knowing that she would drag me out west. Her happiness is enough of a reason for me, even if I do miss the theater."

Jacob laughed. "Yes, my reason is similar. I am eager to get back to her."

Mrs. Schmidt entered at that moment expertly carrying three plates in both hands. "Well, we don't want to keep you any longer than necessary. Eat up, Mr. Payne. Get that energy and strength back for your trip back down the mountain."

She served the men each a plate full of meat, potatoes, boiled vegetables and with the sharp odor of onions throughout.

"And I've got an apple pie cooling for later," she promised. "You'll have to go to the diner for supper tonight and see how mine measures up."

"Thank you, ma'am," Jacob said as he took his first bite.

"Now," Mr. Schmidt said. "I want to be straight with you, Mr. Payne. Watts was only here for a couple nights. And even when he was in Lawrence, it's not as though he sat down to a meal with us the way you're doing now. I'm happy to tell you all I know, but I fear it might not be enough."

"I understand, sir. Anything you can tell me would be helpful."

"Now, I want to be clear that he didn't come right out and say he had robbed a man, but he talked around it and hinted enough that one could come to that conclusion. Seems he came here after Adair where he had relieved someone of just under a hundred dollars."

"Really? He did this in Adair, too?" Jacob asked. "If that's true, that means he's pulled this trick even more than we thought."

The Schmidts looked at each other.

"We also heard something about Mr. Joseph Meyer," Mrs. Schmidt admitted. "We didn't like to believe it, why anyone would threaten a man with his power and reach, but ..."

Jacob nodded. "I think I can trust to your discretion when I tell you that Mr. Meyer is the individual putting up the reward for Watts's capture. If the story you heard isn't true, then he's an even bigger saint than we thought."

"Heavens," Mrs. Schmidt said under her breath.

"Well," Jacob said. "That settles it. If I had any doubt about this man's guilt, it's gone now. I don't mind telling you I'll be happy to get him behind bars. What he's doing isn't just criminal, but it's foolish and immature. If I don't save him from himself, he's bound to get himself shot."

"Wasn't he bragging something about that, Sarah?" Mr. Schmidt asked his wife. "I can't remember exactly what he said, but he certainly seems to think he is invincible. You might be right about him getting himself shot. If he starts mouthing off to the wrong man ..."

"Miss Jones told me that Watts was talking about going to Raton. Did you hear anything like that?"

"If Beck said it," Mrs. Schmidt replied, "you can take that to the bank. She has a way about her that gets information out of folks when nothing else would."

"That's helpful. But you're sure he didn't say anything else to you? I would hate to get all the way there and find out he's gone again. I can't tell you how frustrating it is to know I might have passed right by that cuss on the road here. So, please, if there's anything—anything—at all Watts might have said to you all about his plans or where he was going, I would greatly appreciate it."

Mr. Schmidt shook his head slowly and looked thoughtful.

"No, sir. Raton is the best we can offer you."

The rest of his day in Lawrence, Jacob visited other merchants and citizens of the town, trying to learn any more details he could about Billy Watts. The kid was certainly memorable to everyone who had the misfortune of interacting with him, though each seemed to have the same story. Watts was a big talker with no filter and no sense of judgment.

Jacob could be all that stood between that wild card and disaster.

He was eager to get going and get back on the trail. Though capturing Watts was far from certain, Jacob certainly would have no chance at it if he couldn't manage to find himself in the same town as the kid. He washed and dressed hurriedly, leaving his cozy room and heading down the stairs well before dawn.

Jacob had been sure to pay his bill the previous evening, and assumed he would be gone before his hosts even woke. He was surprised to hear someone calling for him as he made his way to the front door.

"Oh! Mr. Payne. There was one more thing I thought of this morning. It might not be helpful at all, but you did say anything."

"Of course, Mrs. Schmidt. Anything." He turned to give her his attention.

"Well, of course, I heard this from Mrs. Barnes who heard it from Mrs. Arias who heard it from her husband, so it might not be exactly correct, but it seems Billy Watts has ... oh, what do you boys call it? A tell?"

Jacob smiled and leaned forward across the desk. "Tell me everything you heard."

# CHAPTER SIX

Even leaving at dawn, it still took Jacob another day and a half to travel through the territory back to Raton. With every step Blaze carried him, Jacob was afraid that he might miss Billy Watts again. All this traveling back and forth was taking so much time and every day was another chance that he could get into another losing game and take his temper out on his opponent.

As he traveled, Jacob turned over in his mind the small detail that Mrs. Schmidt had divulged to him. In the almost-year that Jacob had been a bounty hunter, he had found that the women he spoke to tended to retain more details and offer more helpful tidbits than the men. Though it was true that the round-about way she had obtained the detail might have allowed for some miscommunication, the very fact that it was so detailed pointed to its authenticity.

Jacob hoped he would have no reason to have to use knowledge of Watts's tell against him, but he'd keep that ace up his sleeve just in case.

Doing his best not to push Blaze too hard, Jacob arrived in Raton about mid-afternoon and took the horse straight to the livery for another good long rest. Maybe even a couple days here, depending on how news about Billy Watts shook out. Blaze had been an exemplary mount for Jacob; hopefully the two would go on these treks together for years to come.

Though it was certainly too early in the day to find the wanted man at a game, Jacob still made his way to the saloon as soon as Blaze was settled in Raton. He figured he could spend the afternoon watching, learning, maybe even asking questions from other men who've been there longer. If his experience in Lawrence was any indication, Jacob was certain that if Billy Watts had been in Raton, someone would have noticed.

Easily locating the saloon, The Rat Hole, Jacob stepped through the swinging door into the noisy room. Thanks to the large picture windows that lined the front of the establishment, there was no trouble adjusting his eyes to the light of the room. At this time of day, the bar was full of bright sunlight, casting a clean glow on the men and women therein.

The bounty hunter stood just inside the door for a short moment, taking a feel of the place and looking for where he might want to sit. As his gaze roved over the open spots at the bar, he felt a jolt of recognition. Though the man was essentially unremarkable and unmemorable, Jacob had burned his face into his memory.

And he chided himself for not suspecting this earlier.

There, seated at the bar, chatting with the man next to him, was the bounty hunter Clifford Pierce.

This was too much of a coincidence. Jacob strode over to the bar, and to Pierce, not even bothering to tamp down his temper.

"Pierce," he said coldly. Jacob stood to his full height of more than six feet and loomed over the sitting man. "There must be another reason I find you here. I know you didn't lie to my face when you told me you wouldn't bother going after Billy Watts."

Pierce turned toward Jacob slowly and deliberately and looked up at him.

"I honestly didn't think I'd see you here, Payne," he said. "Why don't you have a seat? You must be thirsty from your long ride."

"You're right it was a long ride." Jacob bit back stronger words. His professional calm was second to none, but this man tested his patience. "I went all the way to Lawrence and back. Because of what *you* told me. I have half a mind to take you outside so we can settle this like men."

"Now, Payne, be reasonable. I didn't lie to you."

"You—"

"I just changed my mind. I told you the truth, just not all of it. Hell, I got a living to make too. You can't blame me for hunting a bounty."

Jacob sat heavily on the stool next to him. This was almost too much. "It's a forty-dollar bounty, Pierce. You gotta be spending more than that just traveling out here."

"Actually, it's up to a hundred now," he said smugly. "Word came in not long after you left. Course I didn't have to leave so soon, since I wasn't going as far."

"One hundred dollars?" he asked. "That's

incredible. Why so much? He hasn't killed anyone yet has he?" Jacob was immediately concerned that the kid had tipped into the irreversible state and become a murderer.

"No, he hasn't. Though from what I'm hearing it seems likely. That fool boy is bound to make the wrong enemy, like as not. My understanding is Meyer heard more about the men Watts was stealing from and wanted to settle this sooner."

"So, that's the real reason you're here, is it? Bigger reward, and you heard that Watts has got more than just the fifty dollars on him."

"Of course. What do you take me for, Payne? This ain't a charity. If I can bring this lunatic to justice, protect other people from getting robbed and at the same time fill my own pockets? Well, hell, that's why I went into this work after all."

"Right. Well, I'm going to be the one taking him in, Pierce. Santos specifically gave me the job and I've been on the road for ... close to two weeks now."

Pierce smiled smugly and looked him up and down. "It seems to me you are under the mistaken impression that I *owe* this to you."

This time Jacob could not contain his

temper. The audacity of this man incensed him to the point of outburst.

"What? That you owe me something like your *life*? Do you forget who it was that literally rescued you from the captivity of one of the most notorious outlaws in all of the Arizona Territory? I did that, Pierce. I was the one that made sure you survived, made sure you got medical attention. Made sure you got home. And then to thank me for that, you sent me on a wild goose chase all the way out to Lawrence when you *knew* that Watts wasn't there."

"Hold on, now—" Pierce began, looking chagrined.

"I will not hold on. I am disgusted by your greed and selfishness. I have tried to be patient, assuming maybe things were different where you came from or maybe you just haven't had the integrity that most men have. But I'm not going to do that anymore. The fact is that the Watts bounty is mine and I will fight you off too if I have to. I won't be taking any more lies from you, or rolling over to let you cheat me."

"Well, you don't think I'm just going to back off without a fight, do you?"

Jacob threw up his hands in frustration, but now that he had completed his tirade, he realized how many of the other patrons of the saloon had quieted their own conversations to listen to his. Jacob had said his piece and stood up for himself, and now his anger was abating, though Pierce continued to rile him.

"I see your point, Payne," Pierce continued. "I'm willing to admit it was a rotten trick to send you to Lawrence. But that doesn't mean I'm just giving up on these potentially hundreds of dollars at stake."

"Well, neither am I, so I don't see how this is going to go down. We can go outside right now and settle this with fists, if you like. When you're unconscious you won't be in my way for arresting the kid."

Pierce laughed. "You have about forty pounds of muscle on me, Payne. I'm not fool enough to agree to that resolution. And I know you don't want to risk hurting any of these bystanders by starting a brawl here in the Rat Hole."

"I may not have a choice," Jacob responded darkly.

"Actually, I have an alternative. I don't think you'll like it, mind you. But I do think it's your best option if you're not just going to go home and leave Watts to me."

Jacob didn't respond right away. He hated to

play into this man's plans, but like Pierce said, he wasn't sure what other options he had.

He signaled the bartender, ordered a beer and downed half of it before he gave the other bounty hunter his attention again.

"All right, Pierce. What's your suggestion?"

# CHAPTER SEVEN

Jacob Payne and his rival bounty hunter, Clifford Pierce, had been sitting at opposite ends of the bar in the Rat Hole saloon for more than an hour. They were both after the same outlaw, and though Jacob felt as though he had a right to him, the other bounty hunter didn't agree.

"What's your suggestion?" Jacob had said, after Pierce insisted there was really no other option.

"We play for him."

Jacob blinked, confused, and downed the last half of his beer before responding. "What are you talking about?"

"Well, what do we know about Billy Watts?"

Jacob wondered how much research Clifford had done, whether he had interviewed anyone in any of the towns Watts had been seen in. He stuck to the bare minimum of details, not wanting to show his hand.

"He plays poker and gets sore when he loses."

"Exactly. He plays poker. So, my suggestion is whenever that kid comes in here—and we both know he will—you and I join the game he puts together."

"And … what? Just pretend we don't know who he is? Or pretend we're not bounty hunters at all? What is the point of that? Seems cruel to lure him into a false security before busting him."

"That's exactly what we do. We play against him. And against each other. Whichever one of is able to win the biggest pot, take the most off of Watts and then provoke him into threatening us then has the opportunity to turn the tables and arrest him."

"Every bit of that plan feels dishonest," Jacob said. He hadn't been so tempted to walk away from the entire job as he was at that moment, realizing what his only other option was. "The kid might be making mistakes, but that doesn't mean he deserves to be tricked like that."

"Bah. It's exactly what it means. If Watts is

as reckless as I think he is, catching him off guard like this is the only way to keep him from flying off the handle and shooting everyone in sight."

Jacob stayed silent. No one wanted that option, that was certain.

And now, having agreed to such a ridiculous charade, Jacob had been wrestling over the problem for the better part of that hour, trying to find another option. He needed to discover the most honorable way to assert his claim on the job without having to play into Pierce's plot. It was not even that he needed that cash reward so badly, but the marshal in Tucson had asked him to come arrest this kid for a reason. Though Jacob admitted he had never seen Clifford Pierce apprehend anyone, he certainly didn't seem like the type that would go easy on naivety or foolishness.

God must be laughing at him right about now. Here Jacob was, sitting in a bar named after a rat, while another rat tried to scam him out of his fairly earned bounty. Jacob shook his head at himself. At no time along this journey could he have rightly made a different choice, but he sure was frustrated that he had ended up here.

With the afternoon wearing on, Jacob was running out of time to find an alternative.

He had never been much of a poker player. When he had lived back in Virginia, his brothers had tried to organize regular games, but Jacob had always had far more important things to do. His farm and his family could easily fill more than twenty-four hours in a day. Once he had finally arrived in Tucson, widowed, childless and with time on his hands, Jacob had tried again.

Edwin Hogg had been the first to try to help Jacob become a better player. The two men had made a habit of a couple hands at least once a week, and after four weeks Jacob had lost close to two hundred dollars. Though the loss of such cash wouldn't starve him, he knew there were better places he could be throwing it. The Widows and Orphans Fund of Tucson needed the money far more than Ed did.

That fourth week, as Ed had reached out and started pulling the pot toward him, he chuckled. "You know, Jacob. I'm starting to feel a mite bad about this. You and I both know this isn't any kind of real challenge for me."

"I know it."

"How about you let me make things right— with you and with God, maybe," he winked, "and let me teach you some strategy. You know this game is not just matching up pairs, don't you?"

Jacob laughed. "Yeah, I feel like I heard something like that."

"You gotta let me give you some tips at least. Before you embarrass yourself with anyone else."

"I dunno, Ed. Maybe it's just not my game."

Ed shook his head. "It might not be, but I guarantee there will come a day when you wish you were a better player. Maybe you'll need some quick cash or maybe you'll need to impress someone. Just ... My friend. Please. I can't let you be out there playing like this. You're embarrassing yourself."

Jacob had acquiesced, and though he had never felt the same draw and addiction to the game that other men seemed to feel, he had to admit that not losing all the time certainly improved the experience.

All the same, Jacob regretted not playing more. This was the very experience Ed had predicted, the instance when he would wish he was a better player and use this skill for some bigger purpose. The bounty hunter had no idea how good of a player Pierce was—the other man was full of a lot of talk, and there was no real telling how much of it was based in reality or not.

Coming back to the present, Jacob signaled the bartender for another drink. He checked the time. Judging from what he had heard from the Schmidts in Lawrence, the kid should be there any minute. It occurred to Jacob that maybe there was another saloon or gaming parlor in Raton that he could have gone to. But, no, if Pierce was at the Rat Hole, then that's where Jacob should be too.

In that quick moment, Jacob realized he had one final option available to him. He could preemptively hunt Billy down instead of waiting for him to show up. That ran the risk of missing him completely, as well as of Pierce following him out to the street and trying to stop him. But that was the only way Jacob could think of to avoid a firefight in the saloon or playing a game of poker for a man's life.

He stood from his bar stool and was about to move to the door, when it swung open. The warm sunset light from outside spilled into the saloon, silhouetting the short figure entering.

"I think tonight is a good night for a game, don't you boys?"

Billy Watts had just walked through the door.

# CHAPTER EIGHT

Jacob sat back down and looked to Pierce. The two bounty hunters exchanged a glance as the young man they were both looking to capture sauntered through the door. Billy Watts looked from one side of the Rat Hole to the other, walking slowly into the establishment and calling out loudly for whoever would be up for a poker game. His arrogance astounded Jacob, though it explained all that he had heard about the kid's actions up to this point.

Of course a young man who felt as though he were invincible would continue to so blatantly break the law in such a way. Of course a young man who believed he was the best poker player in five territories would continue to seek out more and more opportunities and then find himself beaten again and again.

And, of course, such a young man would think to solve any minor inconvenience with his pistol.

Jacob took a deep breath, steeling himself for what he needed to do. Though it went completely against all of Jacob's instincts, he had agreed to try to bring in Billy Watts via subterfuge. He could track a man on sun-parched earth. He could prevail in a quick draw. He could even wrestle a man to the ground and physically overpower him. But cunning and trickery were far outside Jacob's usual toolbox.

"Who all wants to try me?" Watts called to the room at large as he settled into a chair.

The two men already seated at that table got up hastily. Jacob wondered how much this kid's reputation had preceded him. Maybe he and Pierce weren't the only men in the room who had heard about this fool.

"I'll go in for a game with you," Pierce said, standing from the bar stool where he had been camped for several hours.

Jacob thought he noticed the man swaying on his feet, by virtue of all he had imbibed throughout the day, but perhaps that was just wishful thinking. For his own part, Jacob elected to stay back and not seem too eager.

"Wonderful. Bartender! Whiskey!" Watts called.

As Pierce made his way to the kid's table, Jacob took one last stock of the room. Guns rested on every man's hip. If Jacob were to try to take Watts by force now, Pierce would try to stop him and there was the chance that every other man present would find themselves in the middle of a shootout.

It was too risky.

Jacob would have to play.

"I'm in," he called, as he stood from his own stool.

Watts barely glanced up to acknowledge him as he sat down at the table across from him. Pierce, however, grinned mockingly at Jacob, as though reminding him that the bounty hunter was right where he wanted him.

Jacob took a deep breath, filling his lungs completely. He was committed now. If he was going to do this, if he was going to let Pierce pull his strings this far, he was going to do it right.

"Anyone else?" Watts called. "It's gonna be a good night. Got a lot riding on this game." He said it casually, as though both wanting the attention but also not trying to make a big deal about it. Jacob could only think that this kid had a long way to go before he was a real man. It was a shame he was squandering his only chance.

"Me," a soft voice said from the bar.

Jacob looked up. He had just sat at the table between Watts and Pierce. He was dismayed that another person was going to get mixed up in the outlaw's antics, and even more dismayed to see the person who was making their way through the room to his table.

A beautiful woman, old enough to have a streak of gray hair growing back from her left temple, but still young enough to have a soft unwrinkled face, strode confidently toward them. She was dressed not as the other women in the Rat Hole were, with corsets and layers and lace and wide skirts. Instead, she wore a finely tailored man's suit. It showed off her hourglass figure without having to boast about it.

"Kate Marlowe," she said. "I've been waiting for a game just like this."

Jacob was so surprised by this woman's appearance and demeanor he spent the next minute distractedly trying to figure out how he hadn't noticed her before this moment. He had been in the Rat Hole for hours, and prided himself on his exceptional observational skills. He could only conclude that she must have equally exceptional skills of remaining unnoticed. There must be a reason she wore a man's suit, after all.

It unnerved him. Jacob didn't like this one bit. And he sure didn't like having to beat Miss Marlowe in a poker game.

"Pleased to meet you, Miss Marlowe," Pierce said, tipping his hat. "May the best man *or woman* win."

She smiled serenely at him, but Jacob picked up a little menace behind the smile. This was a woman who was used to all kinds of nefarious attention from men and likely knew how to handle it.

No, he didn't relish having to play against her at all.

"Miss Marlowe," Jacob said, nodding and tipping his hat as well.

The bartender arrived just behind her, bringing over a full bottle of cheap whiskey and four glasses.

"There's one more chair. Anyone? No one else?" Watts called, as he filled each glass. "Suit yourself."

He passed over the glasses to Pierce,

Marlowe and Jacob, sloshing the whiskey up the side of the glass and spilling on the wooden surface as he did so.

"Cheers, boys," Watts said to the two men both old enough to be his father. "Kate."

He grinned at the woman so wolfishly that Jacob was tempted to warn the kid against her. Between two bounty hunters and Miss Kate Marlowe, Billy Watts had no clue what he was about to go up against.

Jacob watched the other three each take long drinks of their whiskey, while he barely sipped his own. He would have to stay on his guard. His poker strategy itself needed enough of his focus that he couldn't risk letting loose even a little.

# CHAPTER NINE

"All right," Billy Watts said, taking charge of the game. He snatched up the deck and began to shuffle.

Watts was to Jacob's right; Pierce was to his left. Kate Marlowe sat directly across from Jacob and he kept catching her eye. There was no doubt she was an attractive woman. There was also no doubt that she knew this about herself and intended to use it to her advantage. For this reason, Jacob didn't trust her. He was more than willing to give her the benefit of the doubt, but no further.

He watched Watts carefully as the kid dealt, and remembered what Mrs. Schmidt had told him about his tell. That one little piece of knowledge should give Jacob a leg up on Pierce, at the least. There was no telling how good a card player this Miss Marlowe was.

Jacob watched the others, and they all watched him, as the four sat in almost total silence drinking their whiskey and examining their cards.

The game progressed slowly, uneventfully. Players calling, raising. Marlowe trying to engage the others in unrelated conversation. Watts and Pierce both telling stories of previous escapades, each trying to impress or belittle the other. Only Jacob stayed mostly silent as the game went on. He would answer questions when asked, but otherwise kept to himself and kept watch.

Pierce, Marlowe and Watts all had their own strategies about how to dominate the game and read the other players. Jacob just wanted to get through it.

After close to an hour, the pot growing steadily, Pierce was dealing and offered Marlowe one card as requested.

Kate Marlowe reached out to collect her card.

The King of Spades fell out of the cuff of her sleeve, plopping face up on the table in front of them.

Jacob caught the look of shock and fear

flash across her face before she controlled it. He realized this must be why she was dressed as she was. It was far easier to manipulate the cards with sleeves that went all the way to her wrists, no matter if such attire made her stand out otherwise.

Kate moved to sweep up the fallen card into her lap, but Watts had already seen it.

"What's that?" he demanded, grabbing for her wrist.

She deftly outmaneuvered him, keeping her arm out of his reach while still leaning toward the kid seductively. "What is what? I believe I—"

"I saw it!" Watts was beginning to sound hysterical. "You're cheating! You can't cheat me. You can't *cheat* me!" He stood up angrily, knocking his chair over in the process and drawing his gun.

"Whoa now," Jacob said, also standing. "Let's just everyone calm down."

It seemed as though the eyes of everyone in the Rat Hole were now aimed at their table. The last thing Jacob wanted was more atten-tion. Embarrassing the kid—or any outlaw—when they were taken into custody almost always made things worse. And now he had another cheating good-for-nothing to deal with.

"I'm sure we can figure this out," he said as he studied Kate Marlowe.

Her expression flitted between a myriad of emotions. She seemed to be debating her next move and considering any manner of possible reactions to being accused of cheating.

But her instincts were too slow.

Before Marlowe could make her move, Pierce was on her.

"Not so fast, missy," he growled at her as he lunged.

She moved at the same time, pushing back from the table and sliding her chair across the floor. Pierce took two long steps straight for Marlowe, just at the same moment one of the legs of her chair caught on the gap between two floorboards. She was pushing herself back too quickly to stop herself, and the chair tipped.

Marlowe gasped as she and the chair fell backward onto the dusty saloon floor. A couple men nearby moved to help her up, but were warned back by Pierce almost barking at them. Instead, he loomed over the woman, reaching down with both hands to wrap around her wrists and wrench her to her feet.

"Pierce," Jacob said from where he stood on the other side of the table.

"What do you think you're doing?" Pierce

demanded, shaking the woman. "A cheating snake like you? We oughtta—"

"Pierce," Jacob said more sharply.

The other bounty hunter finally looked at him. "What?"

Jacob tried to indicate that people were watching them, without making it too obvious. He inclined his head slightly toward Watts, reminding Pierce of why they were there in the first place.

Pierce huffed, frustrated.

He kept his hand in a solid grip around her arm. Marlowe looked sullen but accepting of her situation. Jacob moved closer so he and the other bounty hunter could talk more quietly, in as much privacy as they could manage with everyone in the saloon looking toward them.

"Pierce, if she did this as a regular thing she'd be better at it than she is. My guess is she's just ... It can't be easy to be a woman out west on her own. Maybe she doesn't have any other options."

Pierce threw a look at Marlowe, who regarded him impassively.

"Do you have anything to say in your own defense?"

She shrugged. "Decide what you're going to decide. I won't fight it either way. I got plenty of other irons in the fire to worry too much about this one."

"Arrogant little—"

"Pierce." Jacob scolded him abruptly.

"I don't like this one bit," he said.

"I know. But, it might be more trouble than it's worth. Let's just let her go. Leave it alone. We don't have to punish her, but we don't have to let her stay either. We got other things to worry about."

"Fine," Pierce said darkly. "Get her out of my sight."

"Yeah, get her out of my sight too!" Watts agreed.

Jacob was grateful to not have a bigger fight, and simply took Marlowe's arm, just above her elbow, and bid Pierce to let go.

"I'll handle this. I'll be right back. Then we'll sort out the rest."

With all the patrons' eyes on them, Jacob guided Marlowe between the tables and out the door of the Rat Hole. Night had fallen, and most of the storefronts on the main street were dark. Jacob hated to let a woman loose into the darkness like this, unprotected and alone, but she seemed like one who could take care of herself.

They walked in silence a little ways, until

Jacob had guided her clear of the line of sight from the front of the saloon.

"Is there somewhere you can go?" he asked gently.

He loosened his grip and she pulled away. Marlowe rolled her shoulders back and straightened her coat. She brushed back a few loose strands of hair and tucked them behind her ear, all the while glaring at Jacob. She didn't do any more than glare, though; this would be a fight she couldn't win.

"I'll be fine," she answered. "Fine. You just get back to taking that poor fool's money and comfort yourself knowing you did it all above board."

Kate Marlowe didn't even look back as she walked off into the darkness.

# CHAPTER TEN

As he watched her walk away, Jacob was grateful that Kate Marlowe didn't cause him any more trouble after being caught cheating at poker. He had plenty of trouble already on his hands with both Clifford Pierce and Billy Watts.

"Is she gone? Now what?" Watts said petulantly when Jacob walked back into the Rat Hole and across to the table. "What do we— Do we start over or... ?"

Jacob and Pierce exchanged another look; Jacob jumped at the chance to steer the kid away from another poker game. If Watts ended it himself, Pierce couldn't hold Jacob to their agreement.

"Yeah, we could call it," Jacob said. "That might be easiest."

"No, no." Pierce smiled smoothly, interrupting him. "No, we gotta finish this game. One more hand at least."

"Yeah, okay." Watts nodded. "One more hand." He set his jaw determinedly.

"But...?" Jacob gestured to the pile of cash in the middle of the table.

"Leave it," Pierce said. "We've got her money. We each put in roughly the same amount. Not one of us is at any more a disadvantage than the other if we just start a new hand with the stakes higher than usual."

"I don't know..."

"No, no, he's right," Watts said, eying the winnings greedily. Jacob could already see him calculating how much more he could win. "Leave it. One of us will get extra lucky."

Jacob set his jaw, determined to win this. Not just for the right to arrest Billy Watts, but also to give the other bounty hunter a punishment for his greed.

Again, Billy Watts took charge and dealt, and again the two tried to out brag each other talking about the places they've been, the targets they've shot, even down to the wildest meals the had ever eaten. Billy Watts was particularly proud of the fact that he had rattlesnake down in Mexico.

"They wrapped it in this ... flat bread thing, with a bunch of spices. Almost too much for me. I don't even know if that's the kind of thing those people eat themselves. Maybe they were just having fun with me."

"Well, if they thought you were a fool they might have tried anything," Pierce conceded.

All the time, Jacob listened carefully and watched even more closely.

There it was. What he had been looking for.

Either Billy Watts had been on the verge of sneezing for a good ten minutes, or he was trying to bluff his way into a winning hand. He kept scrunching up his nose, squinting very briefly, before relaxing his face again. It was clear he had no idea he was doing it. The uncertainty about his cards was written all over his face, now that Jacob knew his tell.

Jacob tried to watch Pierce for any sign of his own strategy, or to see if the man noticed what Billy was doing. That bounty hunter, however, seemed such a whirlwind of talk and gestures that Jacob couldn't make head or tail of it.

He did his best. Lord knows, Edwin Hogg would be proud of how Jacob played this night. But as the evening wore on, Jacob got a sinking feeling that it wouldn't be enough.

Finally, when Jacob was beginning to feel at the end of his rope, and Billy Watts seemed reaching the end of his, he called on the final hand.

Pierce chuckled as he took his turn to show his hand.

"Read 'em, boys," Pierce said.

"What?" Watts asked, stunned.

The bounty hunter slowly and carefully, one by one placed his cards on the table.

He had a Royal Flush.

"Ha!" Pierce laughed triumphantly, and started pulling the cash toward him. He glanced at Jacob, proud of his victory over the kid and over the other bounty hunter.

Jacob was disappointed, but couldn't fault Pierce. He himself had agreed to the man's idea after all. No, what concerned Jacob more now was making sure that Billy Watts didn't follow the exact same path he had followed so many times before. Pierce seemed to be too busy gloating to worry about subduing the outlaw now, this one moment when they had surprised him.

He was going to miss his chance.

"No," Watts mumbled.

Jacob froze. Pierce might have won the

game, but they were still a long way away from having the wanted man subdued. And his arrogant gloating was only going to hurt the situation.

"No," Billy Watts said again, stupefied.

Jacob looked from one man to the other, from the outlaw to the bounty hunter. He was caught in the middle, on neither's side but somehow entangled in the mess.

"I said NO!" Watts shouted.

Pierce froze, as though suddenly remembering what he was dealing with.

"Billy Watts," Jacob began, trying to seize control of the situation. "You are under arrest—"

"I don't think so," he said, suddenly more lucid than Jacob had ever seen him. "No. It's mine. It's all mine."

"Now, Billy..." Jacob moved a slow half-step toward him. If he could keep the kid talking until he was within reach maybe he could still pull this off.

"Hand it all over," Watts said, gesturing to the pile of cash with his gun.

Jacob didn't dare look at Pierce, but hoped the other man wouldn't try to antagonize the kid any further.

"Give it to me!" Billy yelled. "I'll shoot you. Don't think I won't. You give me those winnings and everything in your wallet and we'll call it even."

The room around them had gone silent. Was everyone in the saloon listening to this quarrel, or was Jacob just so focused on Watts that nothing else got through? He took another slow half-step toward the kid, determined to stop this before it got any worse.

"I'll give you to the count of three!" Watts yelled.

"You'll do nothing of the kind," Pierce said, tauntingly.

A gunshot cracked through the air.

"Unngghhh," Pierce moaned, clutching his side.

Watts hadn't even got so far as counting to one before he lost his temper.

The older man keeled over, leaning forward on to the table. A small trickle of blood dripped down, staining the cards that had been left spread in front of him.

"Pierce," Jacob cried.

He pushed back his chair and hurried to the man's side as he slumped further.

"Hold on," he said urgently.

Jacob gathered the other man in his arms and helped lower him to the floor. He needed the man to hold still, so he wouldn't lose as much blood.

He needed this man to live.

While Jacob was urgently assisting the injured man, the shooter was panicking.

Billy Watts carelessly dropped his pistol on the card table so he could use both hands to grasp for all the cash that was lying in the middle. Jacob didn't have time to see what the kid was doing; he was too busy trying to staunch the blood pooling out of Pierce's torso.

With a quick movement, Billy had collected everything he wanted to grab, snatched up his pistol, knocked over his chair and made a beeline for the door of the saloon.

"You!" Jacob yelled to one of the bystanders.

The fat man at the next closest table blinked confusedly at Jacob. The bounty hunter couldn't say how many drinks the stranger had

had, but right now that concern had to be put aside. He was their only chance.

"Help him!" Jacob bellowed, gesturing at Clifford Pierce, bleeding out on the dusty floor of the Rat Hole.

The words were barely out of his mouth when the door to the saloon crashed open and Billy Watts made his way out into the night and the streets of Raton. Jacob ran, weaving between men and chairs to follow him. Everyone else in the saloon seemed in a dull stupor, the result of the beer and whiskey and overall revelry they had been filling their night with.

Jacob was the only one reacting to the disaster.

He reached the door to the saloon and threw himself out into the street. The bounty hunter looked both ways, listened in all directions, even sniffed the air, using all of the senses at his disposal to discover where the kid had gone.

Jacob heard footsteps, heavy running, down around the corner of the next street. That had to be Billy Watts—who else would be running at this time of night? The bounty hunter took off down the street toward him. He almost crashed into a pair of men who were talking only to each other and not paying attention to where they were going, but that only slowed him momentarily.

As Jacob rounded the corner after the outlaw, he heard another shot crack through the darkness.

He ducked instinctively, but couldn't be sure from where the shot had come. He no longer saw Watts in the street. He must have turned down another side street, or ducked into a building. Jacob paused in his running briefly to decide where to go.

Drawing his gun, Jacob knew this might be his only chance to apprehend Billy. The kid could get away again, and now he would know his face.

The moment he stopped, another shot rang out.

"Gah!"

Jacob dropped his revolver in the dirt, and clutched his shoulder as he fell into the dirt road with a heavy thud. He had been shot. It was only luck that Watts had missed a more vital organ. Even so, Jacob felt waves of pain course through him if he tried to move that arm at all. Though he could shoot with his left hand in a pinch, it was far less accurate and far more dangerous for him to do so.

The bounty hunter groaned as he rolled on the ground. He couldn't just lie here. With every moment he took, the outlaw was getting any from him. Jacob closed his eyes. He allowed himself one final short moment to feel through the pain all along his right side, before he resolutely pushed it away with his mind. It would hurt whether he continued lying on the ground or not.

"You okay, mister?" a timid voice asked, approaching him.

A young couple walked hesitantly toward where Jacob was sprawled across the road in the darkness.

"We heard the shot," the young man said. "Let's get you to the doctor."

"No," Jacob said, gritting his teeth.

He saw the two exchange a confused glance.

"Sir," the young woman ventured. "You poor thing. You probably don't know what you're saying, it must hurt that bad. Come along with us. We'll make sure you get fixed up."

"No," Jacob replied, more forcefully this time. "Help me stand."

The young man stepped forward. He wrapped Jacob's good arm around his shoulder and grasped the bounty hunter around the waist.

"Ready?" he said.

With a slight pull, he had brought Jacob to standing. Now that he was on his feet, Jacob felt more in control of his body and of the situation.

"Thank you kindly," he said to the couple. A pulse of anguish shot through him, and he closed his eyes briefly to let it pass. "Do you think you could hand my gun?"

He gestured to the weapon where he had dropped it in the dirt, and the young woman stooped to pick it up. Holding it cautiously—though thoughtlessly—loosely between two fingertips, she handed it to the bounty hunter at arms' length.

"The doctor is just a few streets away," the young man said, pointing. "Come on. We'll take you."

"Do you have a handkerchief?" Jacob asked.

Again, the two exchanged a confused look.

"Something I can use to staunch the blood?"

"Sure. Yeah, sure, mister." The man reached into his pocket and pulled out a crumpled wad of linen.

"Now," Jacob said as he took it from him, "I appreciate all y'all have done for me, but I won't be going to the doctor just yet." He winced as he pressed the handkerchief to his wound, holding the pressure as steady as he could.

"But—"

"There's a man I have to stop before he leaves town."

"The one who shot you?"

"That's him. I've lost track of him, and I'm afraid if I delay any longer it might be too late altogether."

"What can we do to help?" she asked anxiously.

Jacob smiled. "Nothing, ma'am. Thank you. You've done everything I could ask for." He wadded the handkerchief and pushed it through the hole in the shirt the bullet had torn. It wouldn't stay put, it wouldn't hold long, but it was better than nothing.

"Here." The young woman reached back and untied her hair ribbon. It was green, velvet, and Jacob knew from his shopping with Bonnie before leaving Tucson, that such a ribbon could cost a pretty penny. She moved to Jacob's side, wrapped the ribbon around his upper arm and tied it to hold the handkerchief in place. "Is that too tight? I don't think this will last long— please be sure you see the doctor as soon as you can."

"Thank you, ma'am." Jacob wished he had

time to thank these two properly, to buy them a meal or something. But he could feel the ticking clock of Billy Watts on his way out of town and knew he had to move. The best way he could thank these good Samaritans would be by apprehending the wanted man.

"Do you know where you're going?" the man asked him. "You're not from here, are you?"

Jacob paused before answering, looking up and down the street for some sign of where Billy Watts had gotten to.

"What's down that way?" he asked, pointing toward where he had been running before he was shot.

"Um, let's see. Some houses if you go far enough. There's a blacksmith and..."

"The hotel," the young woman interjected. "Turn left at that next street—you can see the corner from here. It's about another two blocks that way."

"That's it," Jacob said to himself.

Quickly orienting himself, Jacob recalled where the other establishments in Raton were in relation to where he now stood. The kid was running away from the livery. He must be going to get his things from the hotel before getting out of town.

Again.

Instead of following at every step, Jacob could beat him to his final destination. Watts wasn't going to get out of town without a horse, and he wasn't going to get a horse without visiting the livery.

He said another thanks to the bewildered couple, spun around quickly and ran toward the livery at the other end of the town. He cursed himself for going along with Pierce's plan at all. He had gone against his instincts and look where it got him—a man was shot, possibly dying, over a measly forty-dollar pot.

But Jacob could fix it.

# CHAPTER TWELVE

When Jacob arrived at the livery, after running back down the main road of Raton in the darkness, his shoulder and entire arm were aching again, almost more than he could handle. The exertion had set his blood pumping throughout his body, and it had soaked straight through the handkerchief that the man had given him.

This late in the evening, there was one lamp burning, but the livery owner was nowhere in sight. Jacob only had a few minutes to find the man, bid him stay out of the way, and position himself for the ambush.

Being half a step ahead of Watts was Jacob's only advantage now.

Once the only other person near was out of harm's way, Jacob cast about, looking for the best place from which to surprise his quarry. The door to the livery had been standing wide open when he had approached, and there was space just behind it to hide him completely. Such a spot would also allow Jacob to be close to Watts when he entered the building and see his approach. He could corner the outlaw without spooking him prematurely.

He hid himself thoroughly, knowing he might only have mere seconds to wait.

The livery stood at the far end of Raton, far enough away from the Rat Hole and the other saloon in town to offer a quiet respite from the bustle of people Jacob had been in the middle of all evening. He stayed alert, listening for the first sign of Watts coming toward him.

The kid wasn't stupid. He might be young and he might be foolish in many ways, but he wasn't completely helpless. He had managed to avoid capture this long. He knew something about avoiding danger.

From his position behind the open door, Jacob heard ragged breathing and running steps approach the livery, but before they fully reached the opening, the steps slowed greatly. Watts was taking his time and looking for signs of trouble.

Through the small gap where the hinges met

the frame, Jacob could sight Watts along the barrel of his revolver. Aiming with his left hand was difficult, and Jacob prayed he wouldn't have to actually shoot.

He watched the kid walking, creeping almost, through the darkness, looking all around him. He was in a hurry to leave Raton, but not such a hurry as to be careless.

Watts took the final two steps and crossed the threshold into the livery.

Jacob held his breath, willing the kid to walk deeper into the building.

Watts looked around, warily. Then he took three more steps. "Hello?"

That was it. That was all Jacob needed. He closed the door behind Watts, blocking his escape.

"Hand's up, Watts," Jacob commanded. His voice echoed through the mostly empty space. Watts didn't even turn to see where it was coming from. "You're under arrest."

"Hell no!"

Watts shot haphazardly over his shoulder at Jacob, the bullet missing the man and cracking the wooden doorframe. Without pausing to try again, Watts set off running from him. He darted from side to side, running through the livery almost at random. But it was the only direction he could go—away from the door and away from his pursuer.

With only his left hand to shoot, Jacob didn't want to take the risk of hitting one of the horses. Instead, he set off running after the boy.

Watts was quick, and lighter on his feet than Jacob. He ducked into one stall, turning into it so abruptly that Jacob almost slid across the floor in his haste to follow. The livery of Raton was spacious, enough that Watts could easily climb over one stall into another, and then over to another row of stalls without ever having to face Jacob. With his injured shoulder, Jacob felt off-balance, and more cautious than he would normally be. He was too slow and too hurt to climb up after Watts.

"You're not going to escape, Watts. Just come quietly. I don't want to have to hurt you."

"The hell I will," the kid called.

Jacob looked up into the blackness of the livery rafters. Watts must have climbed up instead of over. The bounty hunter would need to be sure he stayed between the outlaw and the door. Jacob looked around hurriedly, trying to determine if there was any other way out other than the way Watts had come in. There must be other entrances.

He slowly, almost casually, walked back to

the dark depths of the livery, looking for another door. He didn't want to make too much noise so Watts wouldn't know that the front door was clear. Jacob tried to step on strewn hay as much as possible, to muffle the sound of his boots.

Still looking up into the rafters, careful to not lose Watts, Jacob felt his way along the back wall. There was a wide double door, closed tightly against the night. Still holding his revolver in his left hand, Jacob didn't have any way to feel around for the door handles, so he carefully retreated until his back was against the door. There were the handles—he could feel them jutting into his back and there... He turned, briefly taking his eyes off the dark corners of the livery to check. A heavy chain was wrapped through the wide door's handles and locked tight.

Jacob let out a slow breath of relief. That left just the one opening to the livery. He could make his way back and just wait out the kid.

The bounty hunter began his slow progression back down the wide path between stalls in the livery. The couple horses boarded there watched him with mild interest, though he was careful to keep himself calm and not spook them if he could help it. He stuck to walking on the hay as much as possible and kept an eye out for Watts.

With his trying to stay quiet, his concern for the horses, and his listening for Watts, Jacob's attention was distracted. He had just glimpsed again the now closed door to the livery when he heard a low thump above him.

"Watts—"

But Jacob didn't get anything else out before the full weight of the kid had dropped down on top of him.

"Gah!" he cried, as pain shot through him.

Though Watts had surprised Jacob by jumping down on him from above, the kid didn't weigh enough to give him too much of a problem. While Jacob lay on the floor of the livery, reorienting himself after his fall and pushing back his pain, Watts was taking the opportunity to scramble to his feet.

Through the haze of his pain, Jacob noticed Watts begin to pull away. He had dropped his revolver when he was pushed to the ground, but that meant he had a hand free to grasp at the kid. He almost wrapped his fingers in Watts's pant leg, before the kid pulled away again.

He was going to lose him. Jacob clenched his teeth and made his move.

Though he had one useless, arm, Jacob was

otherwise a physically powerful man. Using leverage from having his back to the ground, Jacob used one strong leg to hook around Watts, and the other leg to kick him over. The kid collapsed in the dirt, one of his ankles twisting awkwardly. In a flash, Jacob had pushed himself up, and on top of the outlaw, holding him in place. Watts squirmed under Jacob's weight, but the bounty hunter held him down firmly with one knee to the chest.

"You're caught, Watts. You're done. Your best option is to come quietly and not make any more trouble for yourself."

"Noooo," the kid whined, dejected.

But he had no other options. It was over.

Jacob had him pinned in the dirt. It would be a mess to try to bind the kid with only one good arm, but Jacob was up to the task.

# CHAPTER THIRTEEN

Jacob had had quite enough for the day and wasn't about to keep charge of Billy Watts any more than he absolutely had to. Though it was after dark in Raton, he dragged the bound, crying kid back through the main street of the town toward the jail.

"You hush, now. Be a man and take the justice that is coming to you. I don't want to have to gag you, but I will."

Watts's sobs quieted a little, though not completely.

"You go around shooting people," Jacob continued. "What exactly did you expect would happen? You better pray and pray hard that Clifford Pierce survives that bullet you put in his belly."

"I will. I know. I'm sorry. I know."

"Sorry doesn't matter now. Save it for the judge."

Jacob had arrived in front of the Raton jail and was more relieved than he wanted to show that there was a light on inside. Cradling his injured arm to him, and with fingers of his left arm wrapped around Watts, Jacob yanked his prisoner up onto the boardwalk and through the door of the jail.

A young man seated at the desk with feet resting up on top, looked up surprised from a heavy leather-bound volume he was reading.

"What's— Can I help you?" He stood, straightening his holster.

"Are you the sheriff?" Jacob asked.

"No, sir. Deputy Langston. What's this now?"

"This is Billy Watts." Jacob shoved the kid forward. He stumbled but kept his feet underneath him. "He's wanted for robbery and my understanding is there's a reward offered for him."

"Of course. Right. That name sounds familiar. I think we got word of a bigger reward just today. Let me take a look at the bulletins we got."

"You do that. Tomorrow. Right now you take this kid off my hands before I lose my temper again."

The deputy frowned. "If you're sure ... "

"I'm sure. I'll be back in the morning to collect and see if you need anything else from me. Right now, I've gotta go back to the Rat Hole and see if this piece of trash has added murder to his list of crimes, or merely attempted murder."

"Murder!" the deputy sputtered, as Watts's sobbing grew louder. "In Raton?"

"You're handling this?" Jacob asked, gesturing to the prisoner and ignoring the deputy's question.

He nodded. "I've got this. We won't let him murder nobody else."

"All right then. I'll see you in the morning."

Jacob was outside the jail and had walked almost twenty feet away before he remembered the pain and injury to his arm. He paused in his walking to pay attention to his injury. If he didn't take care of it now, no one would. The handkerchief he had been given earlier was completely soaked through now and useless. Jacob ripped a strip from the bottom of his shirt, mourning the fact that this new shirt hadn't even made it one job before being ruined. Using the small width of fabric, he tied it around his upper arm, stopping the bleeding as much as he could.

That would do. He didn't need it to be bandaged up completely just yet. The first thing to do was get back to the saloon to ensure Pierce had been properly taken care of.

When he walked back into the place, he was pleased to find that in the time since Jacob had torn out the door of the saloon, at least one of the men inside had acted. Pierce was still lying on the floor of the Rat Hole in a pool of blood, but he was bandaged and being tended to by an older man Jacob took to be the doctor.

The bartender hovered nearby, a concerned expression on his face, and most of the other men that had been in the saloon were now gone.

"How's he doing, doc?" Jacob asked quietly.

The injured man opened his eyes. "Did you get him?"

Jacob nodded. "He should be sitting in a jail cell right this minute. We're just waiting to hear if he's got a murder charge to add."

"No such luck." Pierce smiled. "We'll have to get him on just the robberies."

"That's good to hear."

"Speaking of robbing ... I think you owe me money," Pierce said weakly.

Jacob paused uncertainly, before realizing that the other man was smiling, joking with him. "Well, I've got the pot you won off him, but we'll have to talk about any more than that. I guess you better live a little bit longer and survive this gunshot, huh?"

"I guess I better."

"Seems like you're in good hands, Pierce." Jacob patted his shoulder gently. "I'm gonna let you rest up. When you make it back to Tucson look me up."

"You got it." Pierce closed his eyes, as though the effort of that conversation was enough to take his remaining energy.

With Pierce taken care of, the doctor turned his attention to Jacob. The bounty hunter was scolded gently for doing so much with such an injury—he had lost a lot of blood—but Jacob assured the man that he knew his limits. His arm was cleaned and bandaged in short order, with the doctor's explicit instructions to rest as much as he could. Jacob didn't have the heart to tell him he wouldn't be resting much till he returned home several days from now.

Jacob exited the saloon, and went looking for the Raton hotel. One more night.

All he wanted to do now was fall asleep. The sooner he could fall asleep, the sooner the morning would arrive, and the sooner Jacob could get on the road again, back to his home and back to Bonnie.

**Lonesome Trail**

Before Jacob Payne arrived in the Arizona Territory, before he was a bounty hunter, before he learned how to survive in the desert, he had to travel west. Innocents in trouble, quirky characters and life-threatening peril are along every mile as he passed from Virginia through Texas to the desert of Arizona.

When Jacob comes across a family that has fallen victim to thieves, he can't just ride on and leave them to his fate. He's not yet a bounty hunter, but Jacob Payne can still hunt down the evil-doers. Tucson will be waiting for him once he brings these men to justice.


Sign-up to download this prequel story for free from my website:


**http://atbutler.com/jp-free**

# ALSO BY A.T. BUTLER

<u>Jacob Payne Series:</u>

*<u>Trouble By Any Name</u>*

*Danger in the Canyon*

*Justice for Jasper*

*Blood on the Mountain*

*Outlaw Country*

*Death By Grit*

*<u>Desert Rage</u>*

*<u>Arizona Legend</u>*

*<u>Fool's Demise</u>*

*<u>Silent Night</u>*


<u>Courage On The Oregon Trail Series:</u>

*<u>Westward Courage</u>*

*<u>Faithful Trail</u>*

*<u>Frontier Sisters</u>*

*<u>Unyielding Heart</u>*

*<u>Wild Promise</u>*

*<u>Fierce Dreams</u>*


<u>Other Western Novels by A.T. Butler:</u>

I grew up in the southwest—California Missions, snakes and constant threat of drought weaving the backdrop of my childhood.

But it wasn't until I moved to Texas a few years ago that the magic and mythology of the American West began to seep into my soul.

I'd love to write western adventures for a long time. ...

If you enjoyed this book, a review on your favorite retailer would be greatly appreciated.

- A

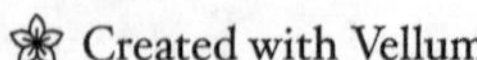 Created with Vellum